The Martian Farmers

The Visitor

Written and illustrated by Matt Loynd

This book is dedicated to my two boys; Dylan and Bear, thanks for your approval throughout the book.

The Martians today were playing with toys, when all of a sudden they heard a strange noise!

They looked out the window to see what and how, and to their surprise there stood a brown cow!

They looked at the cow and saw it had fed, on the flowers, the plants, the grass and their bread!

They tried to distract it by feeding it hay but then they all wondered, 'perhaps it could stay!'

They could have yoghurt and cheese for their dinner and drink lots of milk 'Woo-hoo! What a winner!'

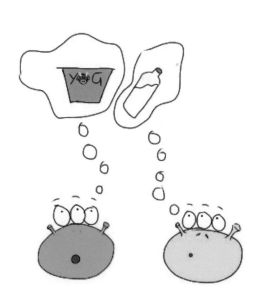

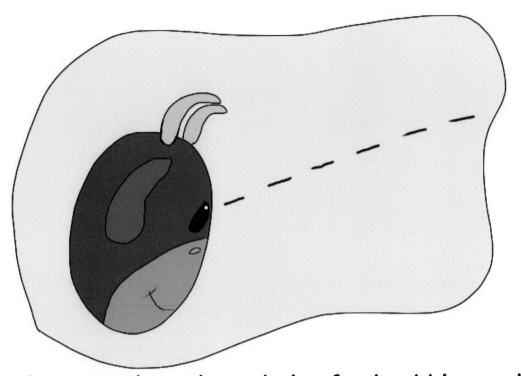

Gally spoke once they cleared the food rubble, and said that he thought that the cow might be trouble,

The rest of the martians agreed with a sigh, as they noticed the cow with that glint in its eye...

The cow was still hungry and begun to look round, for food in the house and for scraps on the ground.

The martians sat down and all wondered how,
they were to see off this hungry brown cow.

Zaggy jumped up and she knew what to do! She walked up to the cow and then shouted "SHOO!"

The cow turned around and stared on in disgrace as it stuck out its tongue and licked Zaggy's face.

Zaggy's idea was a bit too hasty, the cow decided that she was quite tasty!

Idea two soon followed after as the martians sat around and bellowed with laughter.

They would tie some ice cream to some rope on a stick and try to lead it away with a trick.

The sticky dessert was now complete and the ice cream was dangled before the cow's feet

The cow looked down and gave out a "moo!" as it trampled the ice cream and turned it to goo!

Idea two wasn't all that slick, the cow didn't fall for the ice cream trick!

The food or the scaring wasn't doing the job, they needed to get rid of this huge brown cow blob!

So they thought long and hard for the final attempt, Solly said **launch it!!!**....they knew what that meant!

They needed some things to make a huge blaster, if they got this wrong it could prove a disaster!

The martians buzzed round and found lots of things, from cylinder tubes to inflatable rings,

They needed some stuff to make the ka-boom, that very moment Dilly burst into the room.

"I've got it" he burst out, he sounded excited..."balloons from the barn will get this ignited!"

They now had the things to make the huge blaster,
they all lent a hand to make it loads faster.

The tube was made under the shiny moon then
they stuffed it half full with all the balloons!

By the morning the cannon was all fully done, the cow
was to go, now for the fun!

They taped an inflatable around the brown cow
to soften the landing, "so what happens now?"

Tolly threw in some food from his pocket and the cow leaped in the tube as quick as a rocket!

Everything now was all fully set, just one thing to do and without a regret.

The martians all pulled out a pin with a grin and poked in the tube at the balloons hid within

The martians gazed on all full of smiles as the cow blasted out and travelled for miles!!

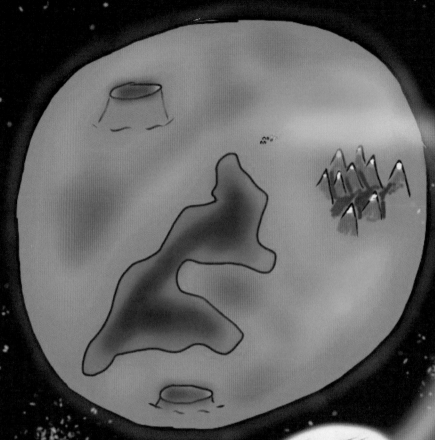

The cow looked down to the ground as he as he darted all around the planet to land back where he started!

The martians looked up and shrieked an alarm as the huge flying cow crashed back down on the farm!

They all looked around and sighed in dismay as they realised the cow was now here to stay.

They looked at the cow and the cow looked at them then the cow mooed out an enormous "AGAIN!!!"

Printed in Great Britain
by Amazon

14498165R00016